# THE MOVIE TELLER

*Hernán Rivera Letelier*

# THE MOVIE TELLER

*Translated from the Spanish by*
*Margaret Jull Costa*

MACLEHOSE PRESS
QUERCUS · LONDON

First published as *La contadora de películas*
by Aguilar Chilena de Ediciones, S.A. (Alfaguara), Chile, in 2009

First published in Great Britain in 2023 by

MacLehose Press
An imprint of Quercus Editions Limited
Carmelite House
50 Victoria Embankment
London EC4Y 0DZ

An Hachette UK company

A CIP catalogue record for this book is available
from the British Library.

ISBN (MMP) 978 1 78087 053 3
ISBN (Ebook) 978 1 78087 054 0

10 9 8 7 6 5 4 3 2 1

Designed and typeset in Minion by CC Book Production
Printed and bound in Great Britain by Clays Ltd, Elcograf S.p.A.

Papers used by Quercus Books are from well-managed forests and other responsible sources.

*For Claudio Labarca, the Bear,*
*who had a cousin who told movies*

"We are such stuff as dreams are made on."

*The Tempest*, William Shakespeare


"We are such stuff as movies are made of."

Hada Delcine (the Cinema Fairy)

# 1

In our house, money rode on horseback while we went on foot, so, whenever a movie was announced at the Oficina,* my father – his choice of movie depending solely on which actor or actress was in the starring role – would somehow scrape together enough money to buy just one ticket and then send me off to the cinema.

Later, when I got back, I had to tell the movie to the rest of the family, gathered together in the living room.

---

* The Oficina – the Office – was the name given to the saltpetre works and to the adjoining settlement or camp.

# 2

After seeing the movie, it was great to come home and find my father and my brothers – with hair neatly combed and in their best clothes – all waiting for me and sitting in a row as if they really were at the cinema.

My father would sit in our only armchair with a Bolivian blanket over his knees, and that was our equivalent of the stalls. Beside him, on the floor, were his bottle of red wine and the household's one remaining glass. The gallery was the long wooden bench where my brothers sat ranked by age, from youngest to oldest. Later, some of their friends started dropping by to watch through the window, and that became the balcony.

I would get back from the cinema, drink a quick cup

of tea (which they had prepared in readiness for me) and begin my performance. Standing before them, with my back to the wall – white like the cinema screen – I would start "telling" them the movie *de pe a pa*, as my father used to say, from start to finish, trying not to forget a single detail of the plot, the dialogues or the characters.

I should perhaps explain that I wasn't sent to the cinema because I was the only girl in the family and they – my father and my brothers – were simply being gentlemen. No way. They sent me because I was the best at telling movies. That's right: the best movie teller in the family. Later on, I became the best in our row of houses and, very soon, the best in the whole camp. As far as I'm aware, there was no-one to beat me at telling movies. And it didn't matter what kind they were either: Westerns, horror movies, war movies, movies about Martians, love stories. And, of course, Mexican movies, which my papa, like a good southerner, liked best of all.

In fact, it was a Mexican movie – all-singing, all-crying – that won me the title. Because the title had to be won.

Or did you think they chose me for my good looks?

# 3

There were five of us children. Four boys and me. We formed a perfect scale in size and age. I was the youngest. Can you imagine what it's like growing up in a household of brothers? I never played with dolls. On the other hand, I was a champion at marbles and skittles. And no-one could beat me when it came to killing lizards out on the saltpetre beds. I just had to see one and, paf, one dead lizard.

I went about barefoot all day, smoked cigarettes on the sly, wore a baseball cap and had even learned to pee standing up.

You *pee* standing up, you *urinate* crouching down.

And I did it anywhere on the pampa, just like my

brothers. And in contests to see who could pee furthest, I sometimes won by a few inches. Even into the wind.

When I turned seven, I went to school. Apart from the sacrifice of having to wear skirts, I found it really hard to get used to urinating like a young lady.

Much harder than learning to read.

# 4

When my papa had the idea of holding a competition, I was ten years old and in my third year at school. His idea was to send each of us to the cinema, one by one, and then make us "tell" the movie to the rest of the family. The one who told the movie best would be sent to the cinema whenever they were showing something good. Or a Mexican movie. A Mexican movie could be good or bad, my father didn't care. And always assuming, of course, that there was enough money to pay for the ticket.

The others would have to make do with hearing the movie told to them afterwards at home.

We all liked the idea and were all equally confident that we could win. And not without reason, because like every other kid in the mining camp, whenever we went to the cinema, we would all leave imitating the "young stars" in their best scenes. My brothers did brilliant imitations of John Wayne's swaying walk and oblique gaze, Humphrey Bogart's scornful smile and Jerry Lewis's vacant stares. And they would fall about laughing when I tried to bat my eyelids like Marilyn Monroe or imitate the voluptuously innocent, little-girl poutings of Brigitte Bardot.

# 5

You may wonder why my father didn't go to the cinema himself, at least when they were showing a Mexican movie. Well, my father couldn't walk. He'd had an accident at work that left him paralysed from the waist down. He no longer worked, and received a miserable little disability pension, which was barely enough to buy food.

We couldn't even afford a wheelchair. In order to be able to move him from the dining room to the bedroom or from the dining room to the front door – where he liked to sit drinking his bottle of red wine and watching the evening and his friends pass by – my brothers had fitted the wheels of an old tricycle to his armchair. The tricycle had been my oldest brother's first Christmas present and its wheels soon warped beneath my father's weight and were always having to be repaired.

And my mother? Well, after the accident, my mother left my father. She left him and us, her five children. Just like that. That's why my father had forbidden us to talk about her at home, about "that floozie" as he disdainfully referred to her.

"Don't mention that floozie," he would say, when one of us inadvertently let slip the word "Mama".

Then he would fall into a deep silence and it took us hours to pry him out of it.

# 6

I remember, when my mother was still with us – before the accident – and we were a proper family and my father was working (and not drinking so much), and she used to welcome him with a kiss when he came home from work, I remember how the seven of us would go to the cinema together.

I just loved the whole ritual of getting ready to go to the cinema!

"They're showing an Audie Murphy movie tonight," my father would say when he got home (at the time, you went to see a movie because of who was in it). Then we would put on our best clothes. Shoes as well. My mother would comb my brothers' hair using lemon juice instead of brilliantine, and give them a parting so straight it looked as if it had been drawn with a ruler. Apart, that is, from Marcelino, brother number four; his hair was as coarse as horsehair, and however much she combed it, it always stood up on his head like the pages of an open book. She would make me a ponytail, my hair tied back so tightly with black elastic bands that my eyes would almost bulge.

We always went to the early-evening performance.

I loved that too, because, for me, the evening was the loveliest time on the pampa. The last rays of sun turned the rusty corrugated-iron roofs to gold, and the twilight colours matched the silk scarves my mother wore.

She adored those silk scarves.

As was usual on the pampa, we would walk down the middle of the dirt street towards the red clouds of the sunset. My father, who always walked along arm-in-arm with Mama, would say hello to all the men he passed.

"Good evening, Maestro Castillo!"

"Good evening, Maestro so-and-so."

I noticed that, although they spoke to him, they had eyes only for my mother. She was very young and pretty, you see, and swayed her hips like the actresses in the movies.

When we reached the corner where the cinema was, we would hear the music from the old loudspeakers, and our hearts would fill with joy. Outside, there would be stalls selling sweets and toys. For her and my papa, my mother used to buy a packet of Pololeo mints with romantic messages on them and for each of us a cone of sweet popcorn.

We were nearly always the first to go in.

# 7

We weren't like the other people who waited for the first chords of the march to strike up – the signal that the movie was about to start – before flocking into the auditorium. We liked to arrive early and wait inside.

I was fascinated by the dark nave of the cinema; for me, it was like a mysterious cave, secret and eternally unexplored. When I went through the heavy velvet curtains at the entrance, I had the feeling I was moving from the crude world of reality into a marvellous, magical universe.

We used to sit in the front row, with our noses almost touching the vast white screen which, for me, was like the main altar of a church. The culmination of this ritual was the exquisite moment when the lights went down, the velvet door curtains were drawn shut, the music stopped and the screen filled with life and movement.

I felt as if I were suspended in mid-air.

That was the climax of the strange spell the cinema cast over me. Over me and over my mother. I realise now that the difference between us and my father and brothers was that they liked the cinema, whereas we adored it.

When the lights went down, everyone would sit up straight and gaze stiffly at the screen in front. Not me. I would turn my head to watch the ray of light emerging from the window of the projection room and travelling through the space above us until it hit the screen and exploded into images and sounds. And often, when the movie wasn't as entertaining as I would have liked (too much talk and not enough action), I would stop watching and instead stare, entranced, at that magical beam of fine, luminous dust. It seemed to me miraculous that a stream of light could contain such extraordinary things as trains being pursued by Indians on horseback, pirate ships on stormy seas and green dragons breathing fire from their seven mouths.

At the time, I thought that it also contained the voices, the sound of guns being fired and the lovely songs sung by mariachi bands. I discovered later that this was not the case. I found out many other things, too, some of them rather technical, for example, that twenty-four pictures – or frames – a second passed before the eyes of the spectators in order to create the illusion of movement. I had no idea what use such information would be to me, but I wanted to know everything about the cinema. That was when I started reading the magazine *Ecran*, which I found in the Oficina library.

I devoured every copy.

But I mustn't get ahead of myself, because that happened after I became a teller of movies.

# 8

As in all saltpetre mining camps, the houses provided a neat illustration of the three social classes: the corrugated-iron shacks of the workers, the adobe houses of the office workers, and the luxurious detached homes of the gringos.

Our house was made from sheets of corrugated iron and divided into three sections. The first was the "living room", as people called it (although we never used it as one). The second was the bedroom with, towards the back, the kitchen and dining room. There was just space enough in the bedroom for our three wrought-iron beds. My father slept in one, my three older brothers in another and, in the third, my brother Marcelino and me.

I slept with my head at the top and he with his head at the bottom.

The names of my brothers were, in descending order, Mariano, Mirto, Manuel and Marcelino. My name is María Margarita. As you will have noticed, my father had a thing about names beginning with M. This, I heard him say, when the penny finally dropped, came from him being called Medardo, his mother Martina and his father Magno.

I now believe that the only reason he married my mother was because her name was María Magnolia. They had nothing in common and weren't in the least alike – chalk and cheese, really. Besides which, my father was twenty-five years older than she was.

"That's how things are in the country," I once heard her comment rather sourly to a neighbour who asked about the age difference.

# 9

When he spoke about the magic of names beginning with M, my father always used to say that the big movie stars were all in on the secret. If we doubted him, we had only to think of Norma Jean, who had been a shop assistant until she was re-christened Marilyn Monroe. Or if we wanted a reverse example, there was Cantinflas, the greatest comic actor in Spanish-language movies, who had triumphed thanks to the fact that in real life his name was Mario Moreno. It was as simple as that. "Don't you believe me?" Here my father would pause and look at you the way an executioner might look at a condemned man just before the axe came down, adding something which, for him, provided irrefutable proof of the truth of his theory, the equivalent of a *coup de grâce*.

"Did you know, my friend," he would say, savouring every word, "that in the early part of his career, when he was just a circus artiste, Mario Moreno was part of a double act with a comedian called Manuel Medel?"

I reckon now that the thing he liked best about Marilyn Monroe were the two Ms in her name. He always said that he wanted to have "a girl child" so that he could name her after Marilyn. "Over my dead body," my mother said. She claimed to loathe "that peroxide blonde who can't even act". And yet it was Marilyn's walk she imitated. And when – shortly before she left us – she learned of Marilyn's death, she cried inconsolably all night.

Since, to my father's great disappointment, only boy children were born, there were no major problems when it came to choosing names until, that is, the arrival of the fourth boy. Then my father could stand it no longer and wanted to christen him Marilyno.

My mother objected, kitchen knife in hand.

Major hostilities broke out, however, when I was born. Apparently, my father glowed with pride when he heard that he finally had a baby girl. At last he would have his own Marilyn at home. My mother refused and even threatened him with divorce. In the end, my father made do with a couple of Ms and they called me María Margarita, a name which, to be honest, I've never much liked: there's an air of meekness and resignation about it; it's a name more suited to a submissive wife and mother.

And I wanted to be more than that.

I didn't know what I wanted to be, but definitely something else.

In that respect, I resembled my mother. She was never satisfied with anything; she was always changing her hairstyle, trying out new make-up, practising pouts and poses in front of the mirror, and repeating something which, as the child I was then, I couldn't really understand:

"Why settle for being a glow-worm, when you could be a star, that's what I say."

And she would furiously wiggle her hips at her reflection in the mirror.

That's why, when I became known as a teller of movies,

I tried to come up with a name more in keeping with my art. But I'm getting ahead of myself again.

Patience, that comes later.

# 10

I must admit that I never imagined I would win the competition to decide who was best at telling movies. My second brother Mirto, nicknamed the Bird, was in charge of shopping and was everyone's favourite. Even I would have voted for him without a second thought. He was always cheerful and chatty and full of ideas, had a great sense of humour.

On the other hand, my oldest brother, Mariano, known as the Caterpillar because of his stammer, didn't stand a chance. Despite being the most intelligent of us all – and, as my father used to say, "more serious than a sergeant major" – he was given the role of cook. The poor boy had started stammering when our mother left.

My third brother, Manuel (in charge of cleaning), didn't even like movies that much. His passion was football; he was a devotee of football friendlies, games that lasted all day, with the first half in the morning, the second in the afternoon, and with a short break for lunch. Because of his habit of making a little mound of earth whenever he was going to kick the ball, he was nicknamed the Moundling.

On the pampa, everyone proudly wore their nickname like a badge; if you didn't have one, you were a nobody, a nothing, a nonentity.

My fourth brother, Marcelino, the Open Book, had the soul of an artist. He enjoyed drawing with coloured pencils. At home, he tended not to say very much, preferring to listen. And his one household task was putting out the rubbish.

Then there was me, and because I was a girl, no-one bothered to give me a nickname. They thought women were only good for making beds and washing dishes – which were my jobs in the house – and for that reason I stood no chance of winning. And yet, there were three things that gave me the advantage over them although, at the time, even I wasn't aware of this. First, I devoured comic books about Opalong Casidy, Gene Austri, Kid Colt and all the other heroes of the Wild West, whereas my brothers didn't read anything. Second, I was mad about radio drama, a taste inherited from my mother, who cradled me in her arms as she listened to the latest unmissable episode of *Esmeralda, Child of the River*. And even my father didn't know about the third thing: when I was small, my mother used to send me to sleep by telling me the plots of her favourite romantic movies, which she never did with any of my brothers.

"They're more for us women," she used to say, giving me the conspiratorial wink I loved so much.

# 11

The first to be sent to the cinema was my brother Mariano, the Caterpillar. He was a complete disaster. They were showing a war movie that day – the Germans versus the Americans – and the only sound we could make out and the only thing he could convey fluently was the rat-a-tat-tat of the machine guns, although he was a brilliant mime. I reckon he would have done really well in silent movies.

My brother Mirto, the Bird, went to see a Western, starring Jack Palance. He was amazing. The galloping horses, the shooting, the shouts of the Indians, the smoke signals. We could almost hear the arrows whistling over our heads – whish! The only problem was that Mirto's re-telling was full of "fucks" and "fuckers":

"Then, when the fucker got his gun out and aimed at the other fucker's head, he was really fucked because the other fuckers weren't going to let him fuck with them like that . . ."

Manuel was sent to see a vampire movie, and although he was normally good at telling movies, love ruined his chances. At twelve years old, he had fallen for the daughter of the owner of the Oficina's best-stocked shop – he was the only one of my brothers who dated girls – and he spent the whole hour and forty minutes of the movie with his arms around the girl, who kept screaming in terror.

My brother Marcelino had the worst luck of all. He was by nature silent – when my mother was still with us, she always used to say "getting a word out of that boy is like getting a cork out of a bottle with a corkscrew" – and it fell to him to go and see *The Old Man and the Sea*, which has almost no dialogue at all.

His telling lasted five minutes at most.

Finally, two weeks later, it was my turn, the little sister, María Margarita or MM as my father sometimes called me. I didn't have an official nickname, but I knew that behind my back some children called me Marimacha – the Tomboy. Not a particularly refined nickname, but as you can see, it's made up of one word beginning with M.

During those two weeks they showed several good movies, some really excellent, but there was no money to buy a ticket. It was halfway through the month and we had barely enough to buy food and my father's daily bottle of wine.

"We'll have to wait until I get my pension," he said. And on that very day, what do you think they were showing? *Ben-Hur*: the movie everyone was longing to see.

My brothers were furious.

They all wanted to go to the cinema. "At least send Mario," they said, because he was deemed to have been the best movie teller so far. But my father, who was a fair man, refused.

"No, it's María Margarita's turn, and María Margarita will go. And that's that."

# 12

The movie lasted three whole hours. I cried even more than Sara García, that veteran star of Mexican movies.

I had never enjoyed a film so much. Later on, I learned that, as well as being very long, it had also been the most expensive movie ever made. And had won eleven Oscars. Besides, Charlton Heston was one of my favourite actors.

I arrived home with my eyes still red from crying. The rest of the family were waiting for me expectantly. I drank a cup of tea in silence, then stood up in front of them and, without a tremor, began my account of the movie.

Something seemed to take me over.

While I was telling the movie, I was altered, transformed; through my facial expressions, gestures and voice,

I became each of the characters in turn. That afternoon, I was the young Ben-Hur. I was Messala, the bad guy of the movie. I was the two leper women Jesus healed.

I was Jesus Himself.

I wasn't telling the movie, I was performing it. More than that, I was living it. My father and my brothers listened and looked, open-mouthed.

"The girl's a real artist," said my father when, drained and exhausted, I finished my performance.

He and my brothers were utterly transfixed.

And their eyes were filled with tears.

# 13

That performance was not enough to win me the title though. My father declared a draw: my brother Mirto and I had clearly been the best. And so, as a committed democrat, he declared that the matter should be decided by secret ballot.

Mirto would be candidate number 1.

I would be candidate number 2.

They cut up four pieces of paper all exactly the same size and distributed them among the voters (we candidates did not have the right to vote). They each wrote down the number of their chosen candidate and then placed their ballot paper in a paper cone.

Then came the counting.

Two votes for my brother and two for me (I guessed that my father and Marcelino had voted for me). To break the deadlock, my father decided to do what was only just and reasonable: Mirto and I would go together to see the next movie, and the one who gave the best account of the movie afterwards would be the winner.

It fell to us to see a Mexican movie full of songs: it was called *Guitars at Midnight*, and its stars were none other than Miguel Aceves Mejía and Lola Beltrán, two of the voices you were most likely to hear in the cantinas on the pampa. My brother was the first to perform and he did so with his usual wit and fluency. He was particularly good at imitating a Mexican accent.

I was equally skilled at putting on a Mexican voice (I'd seen a lot of Mexican movies in my short life) and at telling the story – with descriptions of landscapes and everything – but I sang the songs as well (I'd heard them blaring forth from the loudspeakers outside the cantinas so often that I knew them by heart). My father and my brothers, who had never heard me sing, were amazed that I could sing at all and even more amazed that I could do it so well.

It surprised me too.

My father was astonished, especially when I sang "*No soy monedita de oro*" – "I'm no angel" – one of his favourite songs. The confirmed democrat promptly forgot all about votes and plebiscites and declared me the out-and-out winner.

"And that's my final word!" he roared when Mirto timidly protested.

# 14

And that's how I became the household's official movie teller.

From then on, I stopped playing marbles and no longer went with my brothers to the saltpetre beds to kill lizards. Instead, on the days when I didn't go to the cinema – because there wasn't enough money or because my father didn't recognise the names of the stars – I would stay at home practising different voices and expressions in front of the mirror.

I wanted to get better and better at telling movies.

At the cinema, I began to notice details that would pass most movie-goers by, small touches that helped me bring my performances more vividly to life: the vulgar way the blonde lover of the mafia man applied her lipstick, a gunman's almost imperceptible tic just before he drew his gun, the way soldiers lit their cigarettes in the trenches so that the enemy wouldn't see the flame of the match.

After a while, no longer satisfied with mimicry and putting on voices, I began to incorporate props, like in the theatre. The first were my brothers' wooden toy pistols, an ancient hat of my father's and an old umbrella my mother had brought from the south and had, of course, never needed to use on the pampa.

Then I began to make my own.

Since I had always done well in sewing classes at school, I spent my time making veils and turbans for movies about Arabs, creating fans for Spanish movies and those huge, broad-brimmed sombreros for Mexican ones. I made Chinese swords, helmets, arrows and various types of mask; the first mask I made was in order to play the part of Zorro. What gave me most pleasure, though, was making and wearing the bowler hat, walking stick and toothbrush moustache of Charlie Chaplin, my soulmate.

I kept all these things in a tea chest next to the white wall, within easy reach.

# 15

One of the problems with the Oficina's cinema was that the projector was always breaking down. Whenever this happened, all hell broke loose in the "auditorium". The audience would whistle and stamp and generally kick up a ruckus, heaping insults on the curmudgeonly old projectionist, who, in turn, blamed the ancient equipment he had to work with.

"Go and complain to El Coño, you idiots!" he would bawl through one of the small windows in the projection room, El Coño being the cinema licensee, a Spaniard who also owned a clothes shop and ran the abattoir.

In the end, the only losers were the spectators because, when he re-started the film, it had often jumped forward several scenes, although that was the least of my problems. Back at home, I had no trouble imagining or inventing the missing scenes.

No, the other thing that happened to the Nojectionist, as he was known, was that he would get the reels mixed up – especially when he was the worse for wear with drink – and the end of the movie would turn up in the middle.

Or the beginning at the end.

Or the middle at the beginning.

Then the film became complete gibberish and no-one could understand a thing.

When that happened, it did rather complicate matters, but it still wasn't that hard for me to make sense of the story in my head and tell the whole movie from start to finish, in the right order.

I think that, basically, I had the soul of a gossip, because I just had to look at the two or three images on the poster – the priest's lascivious gaze, the young girl's innocent smile and the knowing look on the face of the devout churchgoer – to be able to invent a plot, imagine the whole story and make my own movie.

# 16

My talent, however, did not depend solely on my wild imagination. Or on my excellent memory. Or on the verbal flourishes learned from my mother and from the husky-voiced narrators of radio dramas (instead of saying simply: "Then he kissed her on the lips", I would linger rather longer over the words: "Then he stubbed out his cigarette, looked into her eyes, encircled her with his strong arms and pressed his lips to hers"). But none of that was as important as concentration.

Concentration was the main thing.

My powers of concentration were proof against anything: people who went to the cinema solely to talk; screaming children; being hit on the head by the troublemakers sitting behind me; and proof, above all, against the licentious, slightly older boys who went to the cinema not to see the movie, but to try and touch up the girls.

It was a sport for them. If we didn't let them do as they pleased, they would call us "bitches" and go and try their luck elsewhere. They would sit down next to a girl on her own and then, after a while, take her hand. Then they would try to put their arm around her and kiss her. Encouraged by the bolder – or more frightened – girls, some even went so far as to fondle the girl's breasts. Or slip a hand between her legs. (Once, one of the bigger boys – he did it for a bet, he said – removed a girl's pink knickers, whirled them triumphantly above his head, then tossed them into the air; and since it was a particularly boring movie, the audience began jubilantly throwing them from one to the other.)

I didn't let them get away with anything.

What did I care if they accused me of being a goody-goody. True, despite my youth, I had already played at Mamas and Papas with some of my brothers' friends, but I went to the cinema to see the movie.

And I couldn't allow anything to distract me.

# 17

What did cause me problems – serious ones – were any movies containing scenes of marital infidelity. Then I had to make full use of my inventive powers and change the plot so as not to hurt my papa's feelings.

Two years had passed since my mother ran away, but, as my father would say whenever he got drunk, the wound was still oozing blood. For that reason, we were not only forbidden to mention her name, we had to avoid saying or doing anything that might remind him of her. If we failed, the poor man would lock himself in his room, weeping silent, bitter tears, as happened one day when in order to play the part of a flamenco dancer in a Spanish movie, I had the not-so-brilliant idea of putting on a dress my mother had left behind, one with red polka dots and frills that she really liked and which she probably hadn't taken with her because my father had hidden it.

My father was always hiding it so that she couldn't wear it.

The dress, which was just right for the role of *bailaora*, only needed pinning here and there to be a perfect fit. Like most eleven-year-old girls on the pampa, I was very well developed for my age.

Some men used to say, with a lubricious glint in their eye, that the reason we pampa girls matured so quickly was the saltpetre; well, it was, after all, considered to be the best natural fertiliser in the world.

That night, when my father saw me wearing my mother's dress, he turned deathly pale, hurled his glass of wine at the wall (the only glass left in the house) and, spluttering angrily, ordered me to take the dress off at once.

The evening's performance was cancelled and he spent the next three days sulking in his room, drinking his wine from a china jug.

He wouldn't even let us put him to bed, because normally, every night, we would unbend his legs – which creaked like rusty hinges – to put him into bed and, in the morning, bend them again to sit him down in his chair.

# 18

Meanwhile, people in the camp started talking about me. While queuing up for bread at the company store or walking home from school down the main street, I would occasionally hear someone say: "She's the girl who tells movies." But I only realised how popular I had become when I returned one evening from the cinema to find more people than usual waiting for me at the house.

As well as my brothers' friends – who had gone from watching through the window to coming in and sitting on the floor – my father had invited two of his ex-workmates, along with their wives and children. My brothers had to give up their bench and sit on the floor with their friends.

While I was drinking my cup of tea and preparing

myself to stand with my back to the white wall and tell the movie, my father kept boasting to his guests that, even if the movie was in black-and-white and on a small screen, this girl, my friends, will tell it to you in technicolour and cinemascope.

"Just you wait."

I loved being able to tell the movie to a larger audience. I felt like a real artist and I think I gave one of my best performances. The movie was a musical comedy starring Marisol, the child prodigy from Spain. Our visitors were amazed. Not only because of the way I told the story and acted it out, but by how well I sang the songs.

The applause that followed was music to my ears.

From that day on, people began to speak openly about my special talent as a teller of movies and, each night, more of my father's friends would turn up at the house to hear me.

To see me and hear me.

# 19

One evening, one of the guests commented, quite casually, that we should charge an entrance fee, something that would never have occurred to us as a family. I was putting on a proper artistic performance, he said.

"And art, my friends, doesn't come cheap."

And so that night, after he had talked it over for a couple of hours with my older brothers – no-one consulted me, of course – my father found the perfect solution: we wouldn't ask for an entrance fee, but for a voluntary donation.

"That's the safest way," he said, "but first we have to reorganise the living room."

The following day, they set to work. My brothers got hold of a bench and an old chair, which they repaired with a hammer and nails. They also installed a couple of upturned tubs, a beer crate and anything else that would serve as seating. We even brought in the big rock from outside the front door on which, before my father had his accident, he used to sit and drink his bottle of wine.

And it all began really well.

The "auditorium" filled up with children and adults, male and female. Some went to see the movie first, then came to the house afterwards to hear me tell it. They would leave saying that the movie I'd told was far better than the one they'd seen.

Encouraged by my popularity, and even neglecting my schoolwork, I stopped reading comic strips and focussed entirely on the magazine *Ecran* (I learned that *écran* was the French word for cinema screen). As well as devouring every new issue that arrived in the library, I read a whole pile of back copies that the librarian brought up from the cellar for me. I found two sections of particular interest: "Premières" and "Hollywood gossip". I wanted to know absolutely everything about the movies and the actresses who usually adorned the front cover of the magazine.

I felt like one of them.

So much so that I even considered inventing a pseudonym. I was an artist and deserved to have an artist's
name.

A name suited to what I did, of course.

# 20

From reading *Ecran*, I had learned that the majority of famous actors and actresses had made-up names, because their real names were as ugly as mine. Or even uglier. For example, Pola Negri, that great diva of the silent cinema, whose name I had always really liked because it seemed so perfect for an actress. Well, one dark day, I discovered with horror that it was a pseudonym, and that her real name was Apolonia Chavulez. It can't be true, I said to myself in dismay. With a name like that the poor thing wouldn't have been able to so much as flutter her eyelashes.

A further disappointment was the discovery that Anthony Quinn, one of my favourite actors, had been born Antonio Quiñones.

How unglamorous can you get!

Then someone told me that artists of all kinds used pseudonyms, that as well as poets like Pablo Neruda (real name: Neftalí Reyes) and Gabriela Mistral (real name: Lucila Godoy), even singers used them. Especially the so-called "new wave" of singers, who were beginning to be heard on all the national radio stations.

They gave me three examples:

A guy called Patricio Núñez re-christened himself Pat Henry: Pat Henry and the Blue Devils. A certain Javier Astudillo Zapata became Danny Chilean. And a high-school student, Gladis Lucavecchi, became a great singing star and appeared in photonovellas under the artistic name of Sussy Vecky.

So as not to be left behind, I started looking for my own artistic pseudonym. However, after much thought and much inventing and composing of names – some taken from *Ecran*, others from the list of saints on the calendar and even some from an old Bible we had in the house, my paternal grandfather's sole legacy to us – I still couldn't find one I liked. Then, one afternoon, I heard our only educated neighbour talking about me to my father:

"Your daughter has a really magical touch when it comes to telling movies: the word is her wand."

And that's when it occurred to me. "A real lightbulb moment," as my older brother would say.

If I was the fairy of the cinema with a magic wand, then that's what I would call myself: *Hada Delcine*.

Hada Delcine.

I repeated it several times and it sounded good, I thought; it even left a slightly French flavour in the mouth.

And, best of all, there were no Ms in it.

# 21

And so it was that from one day to the next, almost without our realising it, our living room became a sort of mini movie-telling cinema.

We divided the room into two sections, just like the real cinema. We placed any bits of furniture that could be used as chairs at the back, next to my father's wheeled armchair and my brothers' bench – that was the stalls. The gallery became the area in front, where everyone, especially the kids, sat on the floor. The window, which had been the balcony, was blocked off.

Closed and bolted.

Not just so that no-one could see or hear me without paying, but because some boys from the other street – with whom my brothers had been holding stone-throwing fights since for ever – started dropping by when I was doing my movie-telling and throwing things in through the window: chewing gum, spit, water bombs, dry turds.

Once they chucked in a live rat.

We hung a blackboard on the door and wrote on it the title of that day's movie, and what time the show began. Underneath, in smaller writing, we added:

"No dogs allowed."

My father was in charge of taking the money. He would sit in his chair by the door with a shoebox on his lap. The donations were never more than five pesos for adults and one peso for children. At the cinema, tickets cost fifty.

My eldest brother was doorman and the others ushers.

To illustrate how well we were doing, I need only say that children without a peso to spend would take it in turns to peer through the holes in the corrugated iron walls just to see me. And between the end of the early-evening matinee and the start of the late-night showing, which was when I performed, one of the men who sold movie knick-knacks and toys used to come and stand outside our house.

My brother Mirto dubbed my performance the *mati-night* slot.

## 22

The days when I couldn't go to the cinema because they were showing a movie "suitable only for adults" posed no problem for me. Since I had what you might call a "filmic" memory, I would simply repeat the most successful movie of the week. On those days, when all the adults went off to the cinema, the house would fill up with children and a few old ladies, who would arrive fuming about "the filth" being shown at the cinema.

But the best days for us were those when there was nothing on at the cinema. This happened occasionally and for various reasons.

Because the movie hadn't arrived.

Because the projector had broken down.

Because the Nojectionist was ill.

This last reason meant that the little man was so drunk that he couldn't even be transported to the cinema in a cart, which did actually happen once, according to my father.

The advertised film starred Jorge Negrete. The cinema was packed and the projectionist still hadn't arrived. Someone said they'd seen him sleeping off the booze at a table in the local boarding house-cum-restaurant. Then the cinema manager, along with some big, hefty lads, went to find him, loaded him into a handcart and wheeled him down the main street. When they reached the cinema, they carried him bodily up to the projection room where they slapped him round the face, splashed him with cold water to wake him up and forced him to show the film.

Whenever the cinema failed to open its doors, I would opt to tell a Mexican movie, one with plenty of songs in it, because that was the sort people liked best. And then the house would fill to bursting point, leaving just enough room for me to move.

As far as I was concerned, those really crowded sessions

were the best. My father used to say that I suffered from a kind of reverse stage fright. Something like "stage ecstasy" he would say, laughing. And he was right. Because the more people who were there to see and hear me, the better I told the movie.

I just loved the applause at the end!

By then, I had started bowing, as actresses do at the theatre – which, of course, I had only seen in movies. While the people were applauding, I would run into the next room, wait for a moment, take a deep breath, then run back in, making that deep bow I so enjoyed.

My audience sometimes called me back three times.

# 23

After those performances, the applause continued to echo around in my head all night, so much so that I couldn't sleep. As I lay there awake, I would think about my mother and weep silently beneath the blankets. When she deserted us, my brother started stammering and I got infested with white lice. The neighbours said white lice only appeared in cases of extreme grief. And given that I was grieving for my mother, I started eating the lice out of love for her.

That's how much I loved her.

That's how much I missed her.

How proud she would be now, I told myself, if she could see how people listened to me and applauded!

Would she receive such applause after her dances?

Would she have changed her name for something more artistic? Would she still be wearing those lovely silk scarves? Sobbing beneath the covers, I imagined her dancing half-naked on a stage lit by flashing coloured lights. It was around that time that I overheard some women in the bread queue talking, saying that my mother had gone off to work as a dancer in some variety show.

According to them, "that silly idiot Magnolia" had been sweet-talked by the director of a travelling variety show that passed through the Oficina, and he had carried her off to the capital, promising to make her a star. What I didn't quite understand was something else that one of the women said, with a knowing wink: that several widowers had been left mourning her departure, and that the saddest of all was the administrator.

My mother was twenty-six when she left. And despite having had five children one after the other (she had the first when she was fourteen), she still had an enviable figure. I remember this clearly because, on various occasions, when we were alone in the house, I had watched her prancing about in her underwear in front of the mirror.

And yet her face was gradually fading, the way the face of an actress does when she hasn't appeared in any movies for a while. The other thing was that, after seeing and telling so many movies, I often got them confused with real life. I found it hard to remember if I had actually experienced something or merely seen it projected on the screen. Or dreamed it. Because sometimes I even confused my own dreams with scenes from the movies.

The same thing was happening with my most precious memories of my mother. The images of the few happy times I had spent with her were disappearing from my memory, like scenes from an old film.

In black and white.

And silent.

# 24

I read something somewhere – probably written by some famous author – that life is made of the same stuff as dreams. Well, I would say that life could easily be made of the same stuff as movies.

Telling a movie is like telling a dream.

Telling a life is like telling a dream or a movie.

# 25

Meanwhile, my fame continued to grow. So much so that people started asking me to go to their homes to tell movies, especially the office workers and the shopkeepers, who were the richest people in the camp. Anyway, since the money earned from my performances was now enough to allow ourselves a few little luxuries, like buying soft drinks to have with lunch and sending me to the cinema almost every day – although most of my earnings went on my father's bottles of wine, which increased visibly in both quantity and quality – someone, I don't know who, had the idea of having some business cards printed.

With gold edging and in fancy writing:

Hada Delcine
Movie Teller

And that was when misfortune struck.

# 26

The first person to engage me was Doña Mercedes Morales, the seamstress who lived on the square, one of the nicest women I have ever met. Señora Mercedes asked me to tell her the movie *La Violetera* – *The Seller of Violets* – starring Sara Montiel and Raf Vallone, which had been shown just a week before at the cinema. She hadn't been able to see it because she'd had to go down to the port to buy cotton thread and buttons.

I could remember it perfectly. And I knew the title song by heart, because they were always playing it on the radio. And the evening I sang it at home, I had received the biggest round of applause of my burgeoning career.

So that day, after lunch, I set off to the seamstress's

house. On my father's orders, my brother Mirto helped me carry the tea chest containing all my Spanish props. Señora Mercedes was delighted and very generous too. As well as giving me a frilly purple taffeta blouse, she paid me more than I would normally have earned in two days.

From then on, I began to get frequent invitations to other houses.

These almost always came from old ladies and gentlemen who were too frail to go to the cinema. The trouble was that some of them asked me to tell them very old movies or ones I hadn't even seen. I got round the problem of the older films by embellishing the little I did remember with a great deal of invention of my own. Only once did I dare tell a movie I'd never seen at all, and that was when I was summoned by Doña Filiberta, the owner of the camp's only cake shop.

The old lady – who some people said was slightly mad – was dying and wanted me to tell her an old movie (she insisted on calling it a film) starring Libertad Lamarque. The film was *Besos brujos* or *Bewitching Kisses*, and Doña Filiberta rolled her eyes and said that it reminded her of an unforgettable love affair. The scene she remembered most vividly was the one in which Lamarque is shown bathing in a beautiful lake of blue water (the movies then were in black and white, but she said "blue water") and singing a wonderful song called *Como el pajarito* – "Like the little bird".

"Have you seen it, dear?" she asked.

I lied and said I had, but that I couldn't remember much about it, because I was only young when I saw it. But if she were to refresh my memory a little . . . She not only gave me a detailed synopsis, including descriptions of costumes and landscapes, she sang the whole of the song about the little bird. I then cobbled together a story and was still telling it when she fell asleep.

Doña Filiberta, who was ninety-two and had been widowed three times, died two days after my visit to her house. After the funeral, her relatives told how Grandma Fili, as they called her, had said that the movie the little girl had told her "wasn't anything like the one she had seen", but that she had enjoyed it immensely all the same, even more than the original.

"The other one only lasted an hour and a quarter," she had said with a smile, "but the one she told me lasted nearly two hours."

Her relatives said that she had died happy.

# 27

I made these home visits at siesta time, because in the morning I had to go to school and in the afternoon I had to go to the cinema. My father told my brothers that they were to take turns helping me transport the tea chest, which they did under protest, leaving me at the house I'd been summoned to, before going off to play. The agreement was that they would come back for me in an hour, this being the average time it took me to tell a movie. But they always went on playing for much longer and I was left to fend for myself. This was what happened on the cloudy day when I went to tell a Western to the local pawnbroker and moneylender.

# 28

The Oficina was one of the poorest in the region. There was nothing for people to see or do on the long pampa evenings. There was no dance hall and no band to perform open-air concerts at weekends on the bandstand in the square. We didn't even have a "train day", which was a really big deal at the Oficinas served by a railway station.

All we had was the cinema.

But the wages weren't always enough to buy a ticket. Everyone lived on credit, and in order to get some money before payday, most people would trade in their tokens.*

The moneylender's name was Don Nolasco.

---

* Workers on saltpetre mining camps were paid in tokens that could only be spent within the camp.

He was a tall, bony man, as suspicious and wary as one of the feral dogs that roamed the desert. Over time, he had become the most hated man at the Oficina, not just because he was a usurer, but also because he stood guard over the single men's accommodation. He had to make sure that the men didn't take any alcohol or women into their bunk rooms. And Don Nolasco was as strict about that as he was about calling in his loans.

Nothing escaped his eagle eye.

On Thursdays, the day when subs were given out, it was a common sight to see the wives of the workers asking him: "Please, Don Nolasco, won't you let me pay half now and the rest next week? I have to buy milk for the baby."

He didn't care, he was as hard and unfeeling as the saltpetre beds.

I went with my mother on a couple of occasions to trade in my father's token and I saw the man's impassive face.

He really did seem to be made entirely out of bone.

No-one had ever seen him smile.

# 29

The man lived in a dark, silent house in the last street on the west side of the camp. It was a Sunday when I went to tell him the movie.

And it was cloudy.

As usual at siesta time, the streets were deserted, but even more so on that particular Sunday, because it was the final of the local football championship, football being the other thing that saved people from the dry-as-dust tedium of the pampa.

When I arrived at his house with my brother Manuel (my father had dragged him away from the match in order to help me), the pawnbroker came to the door, looked at me long and hard, then asked what was in the box. When I explained, he said drily:

"No costumes needed."

Manuel, of course, was thrilled and immediately carried the box home, before racing back to the football pitch. At first, I thought the gentleman wanted to imagine the characters for himself. And I approved of that. Then I sensed a touch of malice about him, but foolishly ignored my intuition, thinking that I had probably just seen too many movies.

The pawnbroker lived alone. The curtains were closed and the house dark. I noticed how crowded the living room was, crammed with old furniture and dusty trunks. We might not have had much furniture in our house, but at least it was more cheerful than that.

The shelves were full of the things people brought to him to pawn: radios, cameras, sets of china, a length of English cashmere. I imagined the trunks must be full of hundreds of watches and gold rings. On the corner of a sideboard were the tokens people had traded in, bundled together with elastic bands. Everyone knew that the pawnbroker trusted no-one and took the tokens with him everywhere, just in case some worker should suddenly come into money and want his token back. Money rained down on him twenty-four hours a day.

Don Nolasco sat on a sofa. I stood in front of him and started telling the John Wayne movie he had requested and that had been shown at the cinema recently. For the first time ever, my legs were shaking. For the first time ever, I could find no words with which to start the story. I regretted having let my brother leave me there alone.

I was afraid.

That man was like the town villain.

When I did begin, he immediately stopped me, saying that he was slightly deaf in one ear and that I should come closer. Then he said it would be best if I told him the movie while sitting on his lap.

He said this in such an abrupt tone that I didn't dare to disobey.

Perched on his bony knees, I began again. He was looking at me strangely. I realised that the movie didn't interest him in the least, but by then it was too late. That was when the pawnbroker began doing what he did to me. Fear turned my body to jelly and I could do nothing to defend myself. The man did whatever he wanted with me, especially from the waist down.

True, I had done something similar with some of my brothers' friends, in the days when I used to go with them to the old saltpetre fields, but we were just children then. Now I felt that something inside me had been torn open.

When he finally allowed me to go, I left the house feeling half-mad.

I walked home as if I were walking on sponges, and as I walked, I let the coins the man had thrust into my hand drop to the ground one by one. I felt infinitely ashamed, too soiled even to receive the air I was breathing.

As I turned the corner of our street, I spotted my father sitting at the door to our house and tried to hide my feelings as best I could. I didn't want to cause him any more pain. My poor old papa was asleep, his head slumped forwards on his chest. My brothers had left him there, with his bottle of wine for company. I stood looking at him sunk in his wheelchair – useless from the waist down.

And suddenly, obscurely, I understood why my mother had left him.

I remembered, too, that when she left, it had been a cloudy day.

# 30

That afternoon, I went to the cinema as usual. Then, back at home, I told the movie quickly and without the least enthusiasm. I said I had a headache. Fortunately, it was mostly children in the audience and I received few complaints. Then I took my eldest brother out into the courtyard, where we sat together on an old railway sleeper, and I told him what had happened.

Much to my surprise, I didn't cry. It was as if I were floating high up on a cloud of serenity. He heard me out in silence.

He didn't say a single word.

He barely blinked.

Afterwards, I was left with a vague, guilty sense that I should have kept silent.

# 31

Two weeks later, on a Thursday morning, the pawnbroker was found dead in his guard's cabin. He was lying on the wooden floor, the planks of which stank of disinfectant, and his body was strewn with tokens. He had been beaten to death with the handle of a spade.

The four policemen who made up the Oficina's private force – all of them fat and pudgy through inactivity – finally had something to do. Apart from poisoning the occasional dog and glumly patrolling the streets, hands behind their backs, the only actual police work they did was to arrest a few harmless drunks at the weekend and have them sweep out the police station and clean the horses' arses.

The first suspects were the owners of the pawned tokens. The policemen questioned each and every one of them, especially the husbands of a couple of women who were known to visit the pawnbroker's house at night in order to "redeem" their tokens.

All were released without charge.

Since the dead man had no known relatives, the Oficina's inhabitants soon forgot all about the incident, and no-one really cared that his murder remained unsolved. On the contrary, there were lots of people who could barely conceal their glee because, with his death, everyone's debts were cancelled. It was said that even the policemen went around grinning from ear to ear. Because they, too, were in hock to Don Nolasco.

Besides, *The Ten Commandments* was about to be shown at the cinema, and people talked of little else.

# 32

Time passed in a slow and leisurely fashion, as it probably does in all the deserts of the world. I was about to turn thirteen, wore a mini-skirt (recently invented by Mary Quant) and was still telling movies.

My audience continued to grow.

Some children were given money for the cinema by their parents, but they preferred to come to my house, pay a minimum donation and spend the rest on some cheap toy. And a lot of illiterate adults, when the film being shown "had writing in it", opted to hear it from me rather than go to the cinema and risk understanding nothing. And I discovered, too, that some people came to hear me not because they couldn't afford the cinema ticket, but because they really liked having someone "tell" them the movie.

Some said that I was so good at playing the different roles that, in the blink of an eye, I could move from being innocent little Snow White to the fierce MGM lion, and that listening to me was like listening to those radio plays broadcast every day from the capital, because, as well as being able to imitate voices and people's facial expressions, I knew how to keep my audience in suspense.

At around that time, I realised that everyone likes being told stories. They want to escape from reality for a moment and experience the fictional worlds offered by movies, radio plays and novels. They even like being told lies, if the lies are well told. That's why con men with the gift of the gab are so successful.

Without intending to, I had become for them a creator of illusions, a kind of fairy with a magic wand, as my neighbour had put it. My movie-telling plucked them from the bitter void of the desert and transported them, even if only for a moment, to marvellous worlds, full of romance, dreams and adventures. Instead of seeing those worlds projected onto the cinema screen, they could each imagine them in their own way.

I read somewhere, or saw in a movie, about how the Jews were rounded up by the Germans and crammed into cattle trucks – with just a tiny crack at the top of the door to let in some air – and that as they travelled past the grass-scented fields, they would choose the best story-teller among them and hoist him up on their shoulders so that he could peer through the crack and describe the countryside and whatever else he could see.

I am now convinced that there must have been many among them who preferred imagining the marvels described by their fellow traveller to being allowed to look through that crack themselves.

# 33

Months later, my father died.

He passed away one evening at home, sitting in his wheelchair, while I was telling a Mexican film. I think it was when he heard me singing "*Ella*" – "She" – that beautiful song by José Alfredo Jiménez.

How was I to know the song would bring back the memory of my mother's betrayal?

> *I grew tired of pleading*
> *I grew tired of saying*
> *That without her*
> *I would die of grief.*
> *She didn't want to hear me,*

*And if she opened her lips*
*It was only to say: "I don't love you."*

He was sitting there in his chair, with his Bolivian blanket covering his useless legs, his eyes wide open, his mug of red wine in his hand. We only realised he was dead when he failed to give me his usual round of applause as I finished my performance.

The Oficina doctor said it was a heart attack.

Apart from the sadness of being left alone in the world, there was the problem of the house: my brothers and I would have nowhere to live. After the accident, the company had allowed him to continue living there simply because of his excellent work record. He had never had a day off in all his working life, not even sick leave. He worked from Monday to Sunday, including holidays, even Christmas and New Year, sometimes working a double shift if necessary (in fact, that was one of the things my mother complained about). But he wasn't there anymore, there was no older person to take on the family and in normal circumstances we would have had to give up the

106

house. Fortunately, Mariano, who was just a few months short of eighteen, was given a job as an errand boy, and so the company let us keep the house.

A lot of people said it was because the administrator had taken pity on us, but I knew – as a thirteen-year-old with the body of a sixteen-year-old – that pity had nothing to do with it.

I knew it from the way the gringo hadn't been able to take his eyes off me at the cemetery on the day of my father's funeral.

# 34

And so we continued living in the same house, which had now been assigned to my eldest brother. I left school that year – having finished my sixth year at school – and became the mistress of the house. As well as making beds and washing dishes, I had to learn how to cook and do the laundry.

In the evenings, I kept on with my movie-telling.

When I was almost fourteen, the same age my mother was when she had her first child, I became the administrator's lover. But during the time between the death of my father and turning fourteen, a series of events, a string of disasters, propelled me unstoppably into the gringo's arms. He was an old, red-faced gringo with Sinatra-blue eyes (Frank Sinatra was another of my favourite actors), who – as my father used to say about the men he thought had their eye on my mother – had long ago marked my card.

# 35

The first thing that happened after my father died was the tragedy of my little brother Marcelino. One night, while he was playing hide-and-seek in the alleyway, he was crushed beneath the rear wheels of the refuse truck. He died instantly.

How I wept and clung to his little head with his hair like an open book!

Shortly afterwards, my brother Mirto, who had never previously shown much interest in women, fell for a young widow visiting the Oficina, a black widow who drove him so crazy with love that he didn't hesitate to leave with her for the town of Coyhaique. More than four thousand kilometres away to the south!

He left without telling anyone.

He was sixteen and the widow twenty-eight.

Then a professional football club on a tour of the north played an exhibition match with a team from the Oficina. When they saw my brother Manuel playing, they were so excited by his feints and tricks that they carried him off to the capital to train him up in the lower divisions.

At least he said goodbye.

And yet the really sad thing – as sad as Marcelino's death – was what happened to Mariano, my eldest brother. Now that he was working for the company and earning a grown man's wage, he got a taste for the booze. He would go drinking with his friends after work. One night, in the local bar, he got drunk as a lord and started boasting loudly about how he had killed that bastard the pawnbroker. Two days later, the detectives from the port came and arrested him on the spot.

He never said that he'd killed the pawnbroker to avenge the foul thing he had done to his sister. He just said he'd gone there to steal the man's money, but had found only breadcrumbs in that bastard moneylender's pockets.

To complete the picture, at around the same time, the first television set arrived in camp, a machine everyone predicted would be the death of cinema. The arrest of Mariano and the arrival of that television happened almost simultaneously and together they decided my fate.

With my brother gone, I was left homeless and possibly jobless too if everyone's predictions about television came true.

# 36

The day the first television set arrived at the Oficina was a real occasion.

Don Primitivo, who owned the baker's shop, had told anyone who would listen that he was going to the port in order to bring back "a radio that showed pictures". He had even had a six-metre copper aerial made. Anyway, on the afternoon he got off the bus carrying only a huge cardboard box, half the camp was waiting for him.

The burliest of the young men lifted the box bearing the name Westinghouse onto his shoulder and set off, surrounded by a throng of people. Meanwhile, a crowd of children kept jumping up and down on either side of him, trying to touch the box, and the older folk, swept up on the wave of excitement, told him to tread carefully so that he didn't trip, because these contraptions were very delicate. And as if it really were the image of the Virgin of La Tirana, the television reached the baker's shop followed by a positive cortège of devotees.

Or so I was told later on. At the time, I was watching a cowboy film, starring Gary Cooper. When I got home, no-one else was there. I made a cup of tea and drank it, trying not to think of anything but the film I had just seen.

I sat at the table and waited for a while.

Then I strapped on my gun belt and holster with my wooden guns and my wide-brimmed hat and stood in front of the mirror to practise Gary Cooper's "steely gaze". Afterwards, I spent some time rehearsing my "draw": I would whip the guns out of their holsters as quickly as possible, fire them, then spin each gun round on my forefingers and slip them back into the holsters.

I had recently learned that cowboys greased their holsters and polished the gunsights so as to be able to draw their guns more quickly. My guns had no sights and so I could only grease my holster. I would buy a bit of grease from the company store tomorrow.

Then I stood in the doorway.

But no-one came.

Someone ran by on the opposite pavement and shouted to me that everyone was down at Don Primitivo's place, watching his new television.

I locked up the house and went to see what all the fuss was about.

# 37

At the baker's, Don Primitivo, clutching the instruction manual and helped by the site electrician, was struggling to get the contraption to work. He had installed it on one of the shelves behind the counter, between the jars of toffees and the cigarette display rack. I had never seen the shop so packed. Even the policemen, doing their first patrol of the night, had stayed on to see this great novelty.

While the electrician was checking plugs and connections, Don Primitivo, scrutinising the manual as if it were a treasure map, was twiddling knobs and pushing buttons like crazy. Up on the roof, two men were turning the aerial this way and that according to the advice shouted up to them from below:

"Over that way!"

"No, this way!"

"Over there!"

"A touch further to the right!"

Everyone had their eyes fixed on the screen, expecting at any moment to see something like a heavenly vision. Instead, along with an unbearable crackling noise, all we could see was a seething mass of lines and dots, rather like the plague of locusts I had seen once in a film.

After a while, the first images of what could have been a war film began to appear on the screen. The figures looked blurred, like people moving about under water. But we could hear nothing, only the sizzle of fritters frying – that's what the crackling sounded like – and occasionally, inter-mittently, a few snatches of dialogue that thrilled the crowd.

In the fleeting moments when image and sound came together, the audience made a tremendous racket, shouting up at the men with the aerial:

"Yes, that's it!"

Then the crackling and the plague of locusts would return.

I was studying the people crowded around the television – many of them regulars at my movie-tellings – and I could see, during those brief seconds when image and sound coincided, that their eyes shone, in just the same way as they did at my house when I donned my Zorro mask and, with three deft movements of my sword, traced a Z in the air.

# 38

I left the baker's with mixed feelings. On the one hand, I sensed it was true what they were saying, that if television really caught on, then it would inevitably lead to the death of the cinema, but I also felt a glimmer of hope about my own job, because having seen what television was like, I was sure no-one could possibly prefer watching those ghostly images – inside that cold little box – to listening to me telling movies.

I was well aware of the irresistible fascination exerted by that machine on anyone who watched it, but I knew, too, that once the novelty had worn thin, they would come to their senses and shake off the spell they were under just as dogs shake off water and would then return to the cinema and to my living room.

I would go back to telling movies again.

The telly – as some people were already familiarly calling it – was rather like a new piece of chewing gum: once you had chewed it for a while, it tasted of nothing and you spat it out.

It was just a matter of time.

# 39

The television arrived a week after my brother was arrested. One Monday morning, when I was beginning to wonder why no-one from the company had come to tell me to vacate the house, the administrator's red face appeared, framed in the window.

Although on the pampa it's usually sunny every day of the year, that was one of those rare cloudy mornings. By then, I was convinced that bad things always happened to me on cloudy days. My father often quoted his grandmother's saying: "Spiders only spin their webs on cloudy days." Well, if that was true, my bad luck was clearly a particularly hard-working spider.

When the gringo appeared at the window and called

to me in his funny foreign accent, I was wearing a dress belonging to my mother, the one with red polka dots and frills that my father hated and which now fitted me perfectly.

I let him in.

He looked at me just as he had at the cemetery. I saw in his eyes the same glint I had seen in the pawnbroker's eyes, when, fool that I was, I sat on his lap to tell him the movie. But the administrator was better-looking than that stingy old pawnbroker. And he had blue eyes. And people said he was rather a nice gringo.

He was wearing a Panama hat.

He was smoking a pipe.

The way he spoke Spanish made me laugh.

He also said that he had been married when he arrived here, but that his wife had taken one look at the unforgiving landscape of the Atacama desert and gone straight back home, saying: "Women here turn to pillars of salt."

The administrator asked me if I realised that I had to vacate the house.

I said yes.

He asked me if I had somewhere else to live.

I said no.

He asked me if I wanted to stay here.

I said yes.

He asked me if I could do anything else apart from telling movies.

I said no.

He stood looking at me. With an expert eye. As if he were studying a race horse. Then he took a thoughtful puff on his pipe and started pacing up and down, silhouetted against the white wall where I used to tell movies. I observed him in silence. When he stopped and turned to look at me again, stroking his chin, that last gesture reminded me that I had seen him once before in this house, talking to my mother. That was in the days when my father was still working.

"We'll see what we can do for you," he said at last.

And I ended up working as a packer at the company store and, at night, I slept in the administrator's arms. And this might not have been the countryside, and it certainly wasn't the custom here, but I was only fourteen and the gringo fifty-one.

# 40

Television swept through the camp like a previously unrecorded and highly contagious epidemic, one that, apparently, had no known antidote.

Don Primitivo's bakery was the first, then the Workers' Club installed one too. After that, it was the Trade Union Club. Then the late Doña Filiberta's cake shop. Then people started going into debt in order to buy their own television. Less than a year later, everyone had one in their house. The workers had the 14-inch screen; the office employees and the higher-ups had the 23-inch screen. The rows of roofs became a forest of aerials, and a whole new jargon began to be bandied about: audio, signal, selector, channel, set.

Television was here to stay.

For the first time ever, there were whole rows of empty seats at the cinema. And people stopped going to sit out in the square. The streets were more deserted than ever, especially when the telly was showing *Barnabas Collins*, a soppy vampire series.

As for me, I would occasionally be summoned by some ancient, ailing lady who didn't own a television, so that I could tell her an old movie. Or I would be invited to sing at the Trade Union Club as a filler at one of the musical events they put on.

On those occasions, even though I didn't get the same loud applause, I would return home happy.

# 41

At around this time, various other world-changing events occurred. Hippies arrived on the scene. Man landed on the Moon (they showed it on television). Salvador Allende came to power. *El Comandante*, Fidel Castro, drove down the main street of the camp (although all we saw was his beard waving about behind the windows of a truck).

In the south, in the village where she was born, my mother committed suicide. She hanged herself from a fig tree, apparently using one of her beloved silk scarves.

I only found out two months later.

Meanwhile, General Pinochet launched his *coup d'état* and many things disappeared after that. People disappeared. Trust disappeared.

The administrator disappeared.

They replaced him with a soldier. And I was alone again. The administrator left without saying goodbye. Some said he had gone back to his own country, others that he had been shot. I had grown quite fond of him. True, he got drunk sometimes and hit me, but he wasn't a bad person.

He even gave me a television.

He was basically a sentimental loner, much troubled by his sterility. In a way, he was like my father: useless from the waist down.

# 42

And then, of course, the Oficina closed. And everyone left.

They wept as they left.

I stayed behind. I stayed here alone. I had nowhere to go to and no-one to go with.

We never heard anything more from my brother Mirto, the one who ran away with the widow. Nor from Manuel the footballer; his name was never listed among the teams of the big football clubs in the capital. Someone told me they'd seen him drunk in a brothel in Valparaíso.

And Mariano is still in prison. When he had nearly served his sentence for killing the pawnbroker, he got into an argument with another prisoner and killed him. He himself was wounded. They sentenced him to another however many years. I was only able to visit him a couple of times.

He asked me not to go again.

It hurt him too much.

It hurt me as well. In his gestures I could see the gestures of a movie villain (he had taken to speaking out of the corner of his mouth). And after he had killed the pawnbroker, he lost his stammer. And for some reason that filled me with inexplicable horror.

The last time I visited him was to tell him the news about our mother.

# 43

I think I'm probably the only woman living all alone in a ghost town. I work as a guide here. I hand out leaflets that give the history of the saltpetre fields, I sell old photos, back numbers of old movie magazines, rag dolls, toy trucks, things I find when I visit the abandoned houses.

Some of the people who come to see what remains of this saltpetre works ask me, astonished, how we could possibly have lived in this arid, godforsaken place.

For them this landscape is almost a province of hell.

I tell them proudly that, for us, it was paradise. I tell them about our lives in the mining camp. No-one died of hunger. And we always helped each other out. At night, we could sleep quite safely with the front door open. The visitors stare at me, incredulous, some almost pityingly. Some even describe me as nostalgic. Romantic. Melodramatic.

A lot of them think I'm mad.

I don't care. On the contrary, when I'm feeling inspired, I bring them to this house – or what's left of it – which is the house where I've lived all my life, and I tell them about the girl who told movies. They listen in amazement. Especially the younger ones. Well, in today's technological age, the idea of someone telling movies seems totally unreal.

In the evening, when they get in their cars and drive off to the cities where they come from, I go back to being what I am: the ghost of a ghost town.

Or perhaps a pillar of salt?

Then I climb up the steps to the top of the church tower and gaze out at the horizon. Every evening is like the final shot from an old movie – in technicolour and cinemascope – with, as a soundtrack, the noise of the wind rattling the corrugated-iron roofs. A movie that's repeated day after day. Sometimes sad, sometimes not so sad.

But the ending is always the same:

Against that twilight backdrop, I see my father riding off into the distance in his wheelchair, I see my brothers following, one by one, I see my mother with her silk scarves fluttering in the wind. I watch them leave just as all the other inhabitants of the Oficina left, I watch them vanish over the horizon as if they were a mirage, and as the music gradually fades, up comes the word no living person wants to read, emphatic and fateful: The End.

# 44

You know the end of the story already, but there's something about my mother I haven't told you, something I find almost too sad to tell.

Today, though, I will.

Just imagine – as sometimes used to happen at the Oficina cinema – that the projectionist has got the reels muddled up and shown the middle of the movie at the end.

One winter's day, when I was still the administrator's official lover, a circus came to the camp. A rather tatty circus, its tent all patched. Among the performers was a dancer. Someone came and told me it was my mother. I didn't want to go and see her. Not from pride or anger, but because I felt sorry for her, for her truncated dreams (like mine), for the pathetic life she must lead in that miserable circus. She would have been about thirty-six then. I was eighteen and working as a packer in the company store, the mistress of a man nearly forty years my senior. A man who would never marry me. A man who, according to the gossips, had been my mother's lover too.

I suppose really we were two truncated dreams.

Which is why, that night, I decided to shut myself up in the house and not go to the circus. I just couldn't. Afterwards, I learned that I had been quite right, because there was hardly anyone in the audience and the show was wretched.

People applauded out of pity.

Afterwards, while the clowns – who doubled as porters, jugglers and magicians – were taking down the tent, I heard the sound of high heels clicking along the pavement and stopping outside my door. I began to tremble. Then someone knocked on the door. I knew who it was. That was how my mother had always knocked. I leaned against the door, fighting my desire to open it. I could hear her breathing on the other side. "Sweetheart, please, open the door," she kept saying through her tears. I was crying too. We were two shipwreck victims clinging to the same piece of wood. The house, the street, the camp, all ceased to exist. There was just her and me on either side of a door.

Just her and me, as if we were on opposite sides of the world.

After a while, she grew tired of knocking and I heard the sound of her high heels moving off. While part of me wanted to run after her, my hand still kept a firm grip on the door handle. I cried for three whole days.

Later, when I learned that she had died, I didn't shed a single tear. It was as if I had seen that film twice already.